Golf Pro

DIAR

Shamini Flint

Illustrated by Sally Heinrich

ALLEN&UNWIN
SYDNEY • MELBOURNE • AUCKLAND • LONDON

This edition published in 2015

First published in Singapore in 2014 by Sunbear Publishing

Allen & Unwin
83 Alexander Street
Crows Nest NSW 2065
Australia
Phone: (61 2) 8425 0100
Email: info@allenandunwin.com
Web: www.allenandunwin.com

A Cataloguing-in-Publication entry is available
from the National Library of Australia
www.trove.nla.gov.au

ISBN 978 1 76011 149 6

Text design by Sally Heinrich
Series cover concept by Jaime Harrison
Set in 13/14 pt Comic Sans

This book was printed and bound in Australia in May 2020 by SOS Print + Media Group

10 9

MY GOLF DIARY

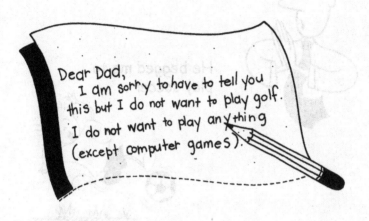

Nope. I can't do it. I can't disappoint Dad.
Not again.

Please...

He begged me to
play soccer ...

and cricket ...

and rugby ...

He asked me nicely to try taekwondo ...

track and field ...

and swimming ...

I WAS HOPELESS AT EVERY SINGLE ONE OF THEM!!!!

But Dad still believes in me.

Our conversation went
something like this:

5

My sister Gemma doesn't understand that diaries are supposed to be private.

She reads mine. And she leaves me notes in them.

I try to ignore her notes.

But then she leaves me MORE ...

and more ...
See what I mean?

If you must know, Gemma ...

One day, one of these sports is going to be the DEATH of me.

And I'd like the world to know what happened to me.

Mind you, maybe I write diaries because there is a writing bug in the family.

Mum writes notes for the fridge.

Gemma sticks notes in my diaries.

Harriet ... errrm, I'm not sure what she's doing but she thinks she's writing.

And Dad's written a book called *Pull Yourself Up by Your Own Bootstraps*. He's up to Volume 2 now!

In his book, he gives people advice about how to be good at stuff.

And it's always at the top of the bestseller lists.

GOOD NEWS!!!

REALLY GOOD NEWS!!!

MEGA GOOD NEWS!!!

Better than when I got an A+ in maths!

Better than when I ate all the cake in the fridge and Gemma got the blame!!

WHAT???

Oops.

Don't read my diaries if you don't like the truth, Gemma!

Dad can't find a golf coach!

The coaches have all heard about how rubbish I am at sport.

None of them will touch me with a ten-foot pole!

GOLF LESSON NO. 1

Dad's bought me some new clothes for golf.

I think he is joking.
I hope he is joking.
I pray he is joking.

He's not joking.

Great. I can make a fool of myself before ever playing a shot.

I just hope no one sees me dressed in this ...

I knew that. NOT.

The next day at school, everyone in class was very excited.

(We're supposed to be making up our own idioms in English. A lot of the kids are really bad at it.)

Dad ???

It will be more fun if you have your friends with you, Marcus.

Maybe Dad's right.

After all, misery loves company.

GOLF LESSON NO. 2

Hulk, JT and James have joined the group.

Yippee. NOT.

Luckily Spot
helped me out.

I felt like a cat that had been hit on the head with a brick.

23

My own Dad is better than me at a sport.
Yippee. NOT.

Hulk hit it down the fairway.

JT hit it into the rough.

James hit it into a bunker.

It was my turn.

I closed my eyes and swung the club as hard as I could.

27

Later, I was hiding behind the sofa so that Mum wouldn't make me wash the dishes.

I wished the earth would open and swallow me up.

I wished I could escape to the moon.

It's no use, Spot. I'm just rubbish at everything... even Dad knows that.

I wished that I wasn't such a disappointment to my dad.

GOLF LESSON NO. 3

Dad decided we should practise hitting the ball out of the sandy bits.

We took turns to chip the ball out of the bunker.

Or at least the others did.

I made sand angels.

Later JT told me that Tiger Woods and Greg 'The Great White Shark' Norman were two great golfers.

In which case, I must be the next earthworm of golf.

37

Four Horsemen of the Apocalypse???

Apparently, 'fore' is what you shout when your golf ball might hit another player.

We all fell silent. There was nothing to say.
The man was right.

I didn't belong on a golf course.

That's where Dad was wrong, of course. Words
can hurt us. I hadn't forgotten what he'd said
to Mum.

When we got home, there was a
note on the fridge.

Marcus,
  I have to go out
for a while.
Please cook dinner.
          Mum.

I'd never cooked dinner before but I'd watched
Mum lots of times.

I decided on stuffed chicken with pumpkin
puree.

The key is to simmer
the pumpkin with milk.

And wrap the chicken in foil, of course, so the juices are locked in.

When Mum came home ...

What are you adding, Marcus?

Pine nuts.

Why?

For texture...

Wow!

You're a great cook, Marcus!

Thanks, Mum.

I may be a great cook, but I'm a rotten golfer.

GOLF LESSON NO. 4

How about losing is ... just a NIGHTMARE?????

About ghosts ...

Or
rattlesnakes ...

Or evil
wizards ...

Or all of them combined in
ONE AWFUL NIGHTMARE ...

ACTUALLY THAT STILL WOULDN'T
BE AS BAD AS LOSING!!!!!

TOURNAMENT NO. 1

I was going to play two holes against the other boy,

a par 4 and a par 5.

I gave my dad a card
I made myself for his
birthday.

Time to hide my
real identity!

So much for pretending to be someone else.

Isn't losing a stepping stone or something?

PAR 4

Dad is my caddy.

That means he carries my clubs and gives me advice.

Hole-in-One's dad is his caddy.

That means he carries his clubs and gives him advice.

The difference is that Hole-in-One is capable of following advice.

He's going to tee off first.

A dog leg?
Spot?
Spot's leg?

Spot! Let me count
your legs!!

I knew that.

NOT.

Hole-in-One hit the perfect tee shot.

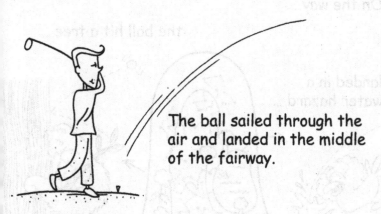

The ball sailed through the air and landed in the middle of the fairway.

It was my turn.

It took me 22 attempts to hit the ball off the tee.

Then it rolled three feet.

It took me another 72 shots to reach Hole-in-One's ball.

On the way ...

the ball hit a tree ...

landed in a
water hazard ...

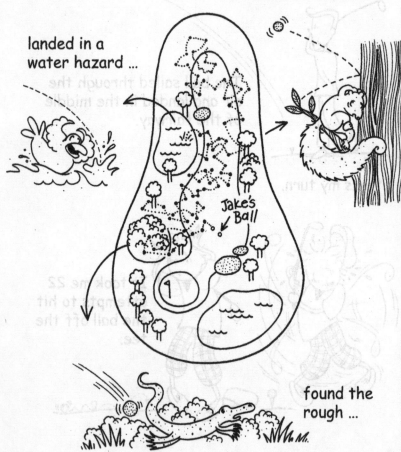

Jake's
Ball

found the
rough ...

Hole-in-One's second shot reached the green and trickled close to the flag.

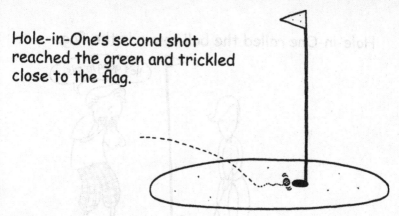

My next shot went backwards.

It took me another 33 shots to reach the green.

On the way...

I frightened some geese ...

I found a rabbit hole ...

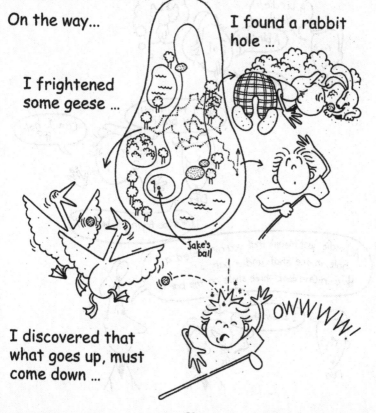

Jake's ball

OWWWW!

I discovered that what goes up, must come down ...

Hole-in-One rolled the ball towards the flag.

54

PAR 5

This time, I teed off first.

It took a while.

A few people in the audience got bored.

Hole-in-One, his dad, my dad and Spot were bored too.

Eventually, I hit it.

Hole-in-One took a shortcut over the trees.

I took the longcut through the trees.

By the time I got to the other side, the sun was setting. It really was a beautiful day.

BUT NOT TO PLAY GOLF!!!!

Finally, we were on the green.

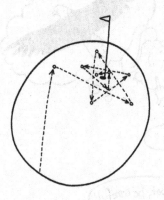

I took a few shots to get the ball in the hole.

At least Hole-in-One was quite a long way from the flag.

There was no way he was going to putt it in one stroke.

Hole-in-One took six strokes to complete the two holes.

Mum let me cook dinner.
I decided on chicken.
A bird that doesn't mean anything in golf.
My favourite kind.

GOLF LESSON NO. 5

Dad is determined to improve my golf.

He took us to a driving range.

You can hit the ball 50 metres or 100 metres or 150 metres.

I hit a pillar ...

Hulk ...

and some poor stranger one level below ...

Dad shut his eyes.

I shut my eyes.

Spot shut his eyes.

Dad tried to be helpful.

But his advice was a bit hard to follow.

Great. I play golf like a robot or a jellyfish.

The only thing missing was ...

Hey Marcus - did you see this?

WEEKLY NEWS
ADVENTURES OF A GOLF PRO

I think I might need to spend an awful lot of time in my room with a paper bag over my head.

Later that evening, I was tasting the lamb stew with dumplings I had just cooked. Delicious!

Be ready for anything?
Really, Dad?

Be ready to accidentally swap bodies
with Spot?

Be ready for an
alien invasion?

Be ready to travel back in time to the Jurassic age?

I invited my friends over for afternoon tea.
I baked a sticky fig and caramel cake with vanilla
custard.

I should be a chef ...   or maybe a maths genius ...

or have the highest score
for Angry Birds in the
whole world ...

But that won't make Dad happy ...

Because he just wants me to be good at sport.

Any sport.

And that will never happen.

NEVER. EVER. EVER.

People always think I'm joking when I'm not.

It turns out that match play means that golfers play to win each hole.

A foursome means two teams of two players taking alternate shots for each hole.

73

There are no problems?

Tell that to the
polar bears, Dad.

Or the orangutans.

Or the whales!

That night, I cooked dinner for the family and a little something on the side for Spot.

I should be happy, right?

WRONG!!!!

You see, Dad doesn't know what good news is. I do.

I think good news is discovering a cool toy in a box of cereal.

Dad thinks good news is discovering that cereal is healthy.

I think good news is discovering that it's Sunday morning and I don't have to get out of bed for school.

Dad thinks good news is that we can get out of bed extra early for more golf practice.

I think good news is not having a partner for the golf tournament.

Dad thinks good news is ... I DON'T WANT TO KNOW!!!

TOURNAMENT NO. 2

Could things get any worse?

Sigh.

83

At least for once, no one is here to watch. My shame can be private ...

Sigh.

HOLE NO. 1: PAR 4

I teed off.

Hole-in-One teed off.

But Dad's shot was fantastic!

It soared over the
trees like an eagle ...

bounced twice and rolled ahead of Hole-in-One's
tee shot.

My second shot
for the team went
sideways ... and
behind a tree.

Dad chipped it
out from behind
the tree.

I chipped it
back behind
the tree.

Dad chipped
it back out
from behind
the tree.

This time I knocked it forward ten feet.

It was an accident. I actually missed it the first time I swung and hit it when I spun round.

YAY!! YAY! COME ON MARCUS! MARCUS YAY!!

Dad landed the ball next to the flag.

We were only six shots behind!

Hole-in-One missed
the putt!

My dad sank his putt.

His dad sank the next putt.

We lost the hole by five strokes.

SECOND HOLE: PAR 5

This time Dad hit the first shot.

Hole-in-One's dad hit their tee shot.

Neck and neck.

Hole-in-One lined up to take the second shot.

He messed it up.

I got lucky.

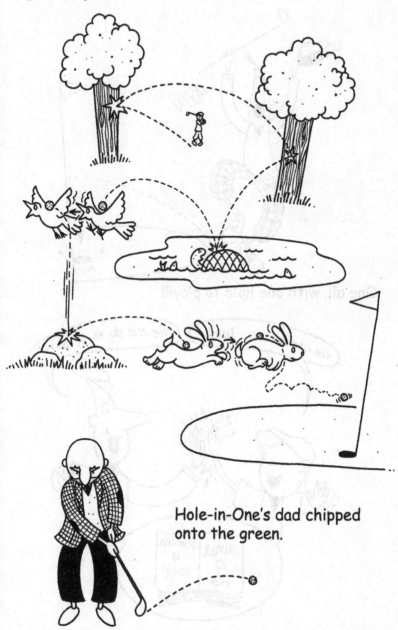

Hole-in-One's dad chipped onto the green.

But then my dad played the shot of his life!!!

One all, with one hole to play!!!

THIRD AND LAST HOLE: PAR 3

Unfortunately, I had the first shot.

And it didn't
look easy.

I adopted the perfect golf stance.

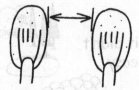

My feet were just so far apart.

My shoulders were loose.

My knees were slightly bent.

My eyes were on the ball.

I drew the club back ... cocked my wrists ... bent my elbows!!

I was ready to play the shot of my life ...

But we still had a golf game to win.

Hole-in-One's first shot landed on the green.

Dad's second shot landed on the green.

Hole-in-One's dad's second shot drifted within two feet of the flag.

101

It rolled forward …

ran up a lip …

veered to the right …

followed the lie of the green …

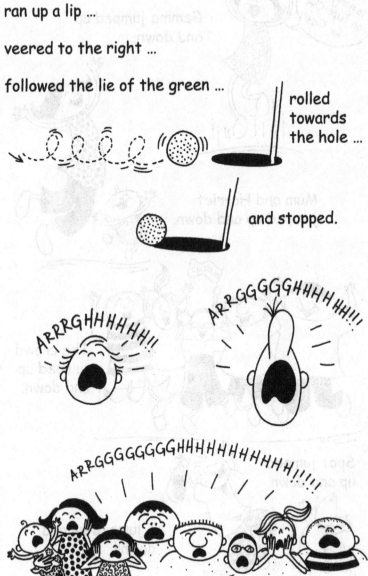

rolled
towards
the hole …

and stopped.

ARRRGHHHHHHH!!

ARRGGGGGGHHHHHH!!!

ARRGGGGGGGGGGHHHHHHHHHHHHH!!!!!

The ball
trembled.

It wobbled.

It quivered.

IT DROPPED
INTO THE
HOLE!!!!

PLOP

YAY!!!

MARCUS

Phew!

Maybe Dad finally realises that I'll never be any good at sport!!!

About the Author

Shamini Flint lives in Singapore with her husband and two children. She is an ex-lawyer, ex-lecturer, stay-at-home mum and writer. She loves golf!

www.shaminiflint.com

Have you read all of my other diaries?

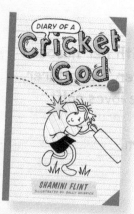

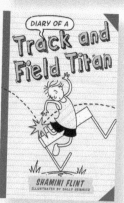